Elizabeth Laird is the author of *Red Sky in the Morning*,
The Garbage King and *Crusade*, and has been shortlisted five times
for the Carnegie Medal. She has travelled extensively throughout
the Middle East, and her son lived for four years in Iran.
She met her husband while travelling on a plane in India,
and they lived together in Iraq, Lebanon and Austria.
Her other books for Frances Lincoln are *A Fistful of Pearls:
Stories from Iraq* and *The Ogress and the Snake: Stories from Somalia*.
Elizabeth divides her time between London and Edinburgh.

Shirin Adl was born in England and grew up in Iran.
She received a first-class BA honours in Illustration from
Loughborough University and went on to win the
Hallmark M&S Talented Designer Award in 1999.
Shirin lives in Oxford and works as a freelance illustrator.
Her other books for Frances Lincoln are *Ramadan Moon*
by Na'ima B. Robert, *Let's Celebrate* by Debjani Chatterjee
and Brian D'Arcy and *I is for Iran*.

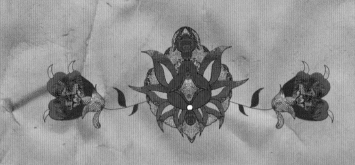

First published in Great Britain in 2009 and the USA in 2010 by
Frances Lincoln Children's Books, 4 Torriano Mews,
Torriano Avenue, London NW5 2RZ
www.franceslincoln.com

First paperback published in Great Britain in 2011

A catalogue record for this book is available from the British Library.

ISBN: 978-1-84780-263-7

Illustrated with watercolour, colour pencil and collage.

Set in Giovanni LT Book

Printed in Dongguan, Guangdong, China by Toppan Leefung in March 2011

1 3 5 7 9 8 6 4 2

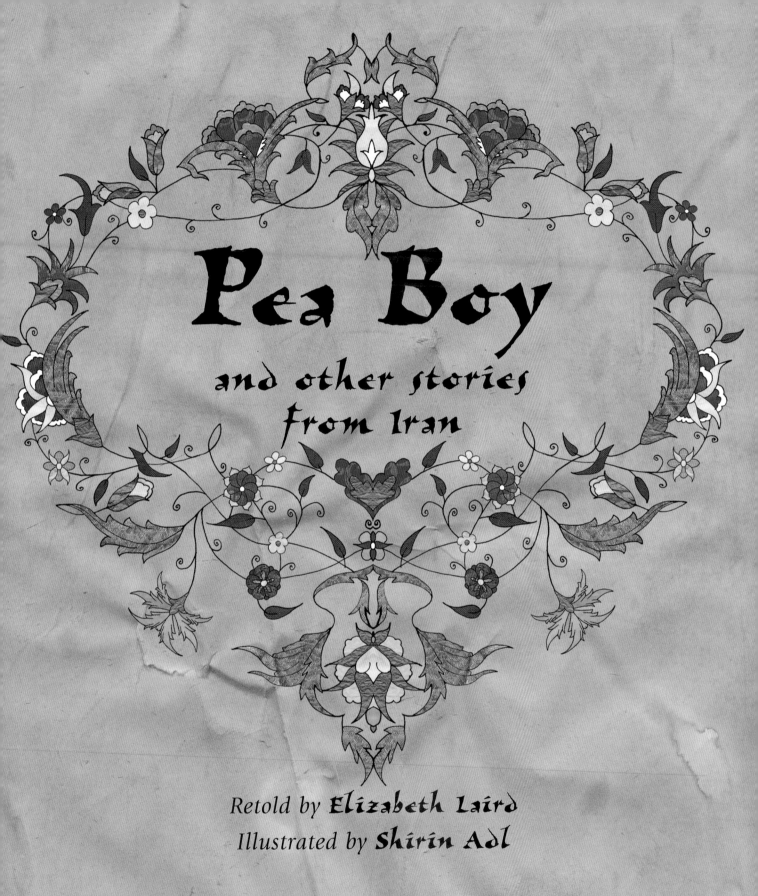

Pea Boy

and other stories from Iran

Retold by **Elizabeth Laird**

Illustrated by **Shirin Adl**

F

FRANCES LINCOLN
CHILDREN'S BOOKS

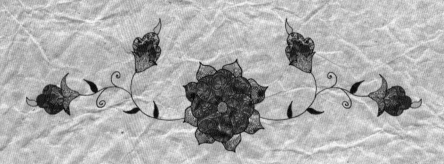

Contents

Introduction

I first went to Iran many years ago. In those days a powerful king called a Shah ruled from the Peacock Throne. He was surrounded by courtiers, and smartly-dressed soldiers guarded him. His palaces stood in beautiful gardens and his treasure-house was full of riches: ropes of pearls, diamond necklaces, rubies as big as pigeons' eggs, sapphires and emeralds spilling out of alabaster bowls, crowns and swords and goblets made of gold and encrusted with jewels.

You'll find shahs and their viziers (advisors) in many Iranian tales, including the ones in this book. There's a treasure-house in these pages, too, which dazzled the Pea Boy in the story on page 38 just as the real Shah's treasure once dazzled me.

I went back to Iran a while ago. There's no Shah in the country now, but many things remain as they were in bygone days. Mountains striped white with snow tower above Tehran, the capital city. Further north, near the Caspian Sea, there are dense forests where bears, lynxes and foxes still roam. You'll find yourself in such a forest when you read *The Cloth of Eternal Life*.

There are great deserts in Iran, too. It's hot and tiring travelling through them. The road stretches on for mile after mile, but every now and then you come to a greener place, just as Kayvan does in *Kayvan the Brave*, where trees fringe a stream or pool. There you might find an old farmhouse surrounded by high brick walls. If you're invited in, as I sometimes was, you'll be offered delicious stews and rice yellow with saffron and the most juicy peaches and apricots you can imagine.

In the cities there are still great bazaars, where shopkeepers like the Pea Boy's father sit in their crowded shops in narrow, covered lanes. These days, you can buy computer games and plastic toys and mobile phones in the bazaar, but more oldfashioned merchants still sell silks and velvets, almonds, cinnamon, saffron and rose-water.

My favourite places in Iran are the gardens where sparrows peck and flocks of pigeons wheel in flight. Spiky, dark cypress trees are reflected in pools of water and students sit between the rose-beds studying their books. It is in such a garden that poor young Mohsen stands on his wedding day when the terrifying monster bird flies down to capture him, in the story of *The Giant Okab*.

Iran is a country full of stories: of jinns and fairies and demons, faithful mice and frivolous cockroaches, foolish young weavers and curious sparrows. Nowadays there are new stories alongside the old ones. They tell of revolutionaries and soldiers, wars, and the leaders and teachers of Islam. But the people who live out these stories, those who tell them and those who listen, are the same – quick-witted, humorous, long-suffering, and generous to strangers.

Elizabeth Laird

Miss Cockroach and Mr Mouse

Miss Cockroach, who lived with her father in a crack above the window in the kitchen wall, was the prettiest young insect you ever did see, but oh, she was silly and vain! She lazed about all day long, burnishing her lustrous wings and fluttering her long antennae, and she never gave a thought to the pots that needed scouring, or the crumbs that waited to be gathered up, or the rips that had to be mended in her poor father's shirt. But Mr Cockroach loved his daughter, and never a complaint did he make.

One dreadful day, Mr Cockroach was tempted out of his home by a dribble of spilt honey, and just as he was about to start slurping it up, the cook saw him, and hurled his spoon at him. One of Mr Cockroach's back legs was broken, and he only just managed to crawl back to safety.

"I can't look after you any more, my dear," he croaked to his daughter, "and you're too silly to manage on your own. Put those good looks of yours to use at last. Rich Mr Ramazan, the merchant of Hamadan, is looking for a wife, and he'll marry you for sure."

So Miss Cockroach made a dress from a yellow onion-skin , and a cloak from the purple rind of an aubergine, and slippers from split almonds. Then she put rouge on her cheeks, lined her eyes with kohl, rubbed her lips with red raspberry juice and painted henna on her fingers and toes. When she was quite, quite beautiful she set off on the road to Hamadan.

On the way she met the grocer, and she waved her antennae at him in a very saucy way.

"Where are you off to, all dressed up like a queen?" asked the grocer.

"I'm off to Hamadan to marry Ramazan, because I'm too silly to manage on my own," replied Miss Cockroach.

"Marry me instead," said the grocer, "but if you spill my coffee, I'll beat you with my broom."

"I wouldn't like that at all," said Miss Cockroach, and she went on her way.

Next she met the butcher, and she smiled at him with her raspberry-red lips.

"Where are you going in your pretty onion-skin dress?" asked the butcher.

"I'm off to Hamadan to marry Ramazan, because I'm too silly to manage on my own," replied Miss Cockroach.

"Marry me instead," said the butcher, "but if you burn my dinner, I'll beat you with a chicken bone."

"I wouldn't like that at all," said Miss Cockroach, and she went on her way.

Soon she met a blacksmith, and she pirouetted past him in her almond slippers.

"Where are you off to, as lovely as a bride on her wedding day?" asked the blacksmith.

"I'm off to Hamadan to marry Ramazan, because I'm too silly to manage on my own," replied Miss Cockroach.

"Marry me instead," said the blacksmith, "but if you break my tea glass, I'll beat you with my fire tongs."

"I wouldn't like that at all," said Miss Cockroach, and she went on her way.

Soon she met Mr Mouse. He was sitting outside his house wearing silver trousers and a cap of woven gold thread.

"Oh, oh! You beautiful creature!" he cried. "And where are you going in your gorgeous aubergine cloak and delicate almond slippers?"

"I'm off to Hamadan to marry Ramazan, because I'm too silly to manage on my own," replied Miss Cockroach.

"Marry me instead," said Mr Mouse. "I'll feed you on honey and tell you stories, and I'll never beat you, whatever you do, but only tickle you under your chin."

"I'd like that very much," said Miss Cockroach, "and I'll marry you as soon as you like."

And so the wedding was arranged. All the cockroaches came in their best clothes, and the mice wore splendid uniforms with buttons made of scarlet berries.

Miss Cockroach loved her husband dearly, but she was the silliest wife that ever lived. She spilled his coffee and burnt his dinner and broke all his tea glasses one by one, and though she tried her best, poor Mr Mouse's house was never properly swept, and his breakfast was never ready, and the holes in his socks grew larger and larger. But he loved his little cockroach and every morning, before he went off to work at the Shah's palace to collect the crumbs that fell from the royal table, he never forgot to tickle her under the chin.

One fine morning, Miss Cockroach decided to wash her husband's shiny silver trousers, so off she went to the stream. She dipped the trousers into the water and scrubbed and soaked and rinsed, leaning further and further down the bank. But the stream was flowing fast, and the trousers were heavy with water. Suddenly they slipped from her hands and floated away, their silvery threads glinting in the sunlight.

"Oh, oh! Come back, you stupid things!" shouted Miss Cockroach, bending forward even further. "Oh, oh! I'm falling in!"

And she might have fallen in and been swept away, but just in time, she managed to catch hold of a reed.

Now poor Miss Cockroach was in trouble, for the reed was only a thin little thing, and it swayed backwards and forwards, bending right down until it nearly touched the water. Miss Cockroach could only cling on to it for dear life, calling out in a faint voice, "Help me! Save me! Oh Mr Mouse, my husband dear! Where are you? Come and save your wife!"

Now, at that very moment a troop of the Shah's soldiers trotted by. They laughed at the sight of the tiny cockroach in her onion-skin gown and almond slippers wobbling about on her reed, but they had no time to stop and help her.

"And what did you see on your rounds this morning?" the Shah asked the captain, when he returned with his men to the palace.

"Nothing, sire," he answered, "except for a silly little cockroach in an onion-skin dress who was clinging to a reed in the stream, calling on a mouse to save her."

Just at that moment, Mr Mouse was scurrying past on his way to tidy up the crumbs in the dining-room, and he heard what the captain was saying.

"My wife! My poor little cockroach!" he squeaked. "What is she up to this time?" And he ran to the stream as fast as his legs would carry him.

Miss Cockroach, who by this time was more dead than alive, still clung to the reed with her eyes tight shut, moaning softly, "Mouse! Mr Mouse! Save me!"

"Oh my little wife, my pearl of beauty!" cried Mr Mouse. "Give me your hand and I'll pull you to safety!"

"My hand?" wailed Miss Cockroach. "But if I let go of this reed, I'll fall straight into the water."

"Then give me a foot, oh star of perfection!"

"A foot?" screeched Miss Cockroach. "There's cramp in all my feet and I can't move any of them."

"Then I'll catch you by the hair."

"No no! I spent a whole hour combing it this morning. You'll tangle it all up again."

Mr Mouse jumped up and down, beside himself with anxiety.

"What can I do, O light of my eyes, if you won't let me save you?"

"Bring me a ladder, a golden one," commanded Miss Cockroach, "and hurry, before I drown!"

Mr Mouse ran up and down the bank, muttering to himself, "A ladder! Now where can I find a ladder? And a golden one at that?"

Just as he was about to give his wife up for lost, he spied the feathery tops of carrots growing in a nearby field. He ran to them and with all his strength pulled up the biggest he could see. Then he set to work, gnawing and nibbling, and a minute later the carrot had turned into a golden ladder with neat little steps running all the way to the top.

Mr Mouse rushed back to the stream.

"Here, my love, here's your golden ladder," he panted. He laid it across the water to Miss Cockroach's reed, and she flicked her hair back and minced daintily down it, holding up the skirt of her onion-skin dress.

As soon as she reached the bank, Mr Mouse caught her in his arms, and what with the excitement and the relief, Miss Cockroach fainted dead away.

Faithful Mr Mouse picked her up in his arms and carried her home to his house, taking care not to let her aubergine cloak trail in the mud.

The next morning, Miss Cockroach sneezed three times before breakfast, and her little body ached all over.

"You've caught a cold," Mr Mouse said anxiously, "and there's only one cure for that: turnip soup, well cooked with onions, and as hot as can be."

So Mr Mouse scampered off to the fields, and pulled up a turnip and a pair of onions, and he dragged them all the way to the Shah's kitchen, where a pot of water was boiling on the fire. He peeled and chopped and dropped everything into the pot, and when he thought the soup was well and truly cooked, he climbed up the side of the pot to look. But the pot was hot, and his little feet began to burn, and he had to hop about on the rim. And the steam went into his eyes and he lost his balance, and down he fell, right into the boiling soup!

Miss Cockroach waited and waited, lying on her bed, snuffling and coughing with her cold. But her dear husband, her Mr Mouse, would never come home again, for he was boiled up with the soup.

When she learned what had happened, Miss Cockroach cried until she thought her heart would break.

"Oh, oh! My dear Mr Mouse! You were the only one who loved me and forgave me all my silliness!"

And Miss Cockroach took off her onion-skin dress and her purple cloak and her almond slippers. She washed the raspberry juice off her lips and the kohl from around her eyes, and cut off her long hair.

"I'll never marry anyone again," she said, "and I won't be silly any more. I'll behave like a sensible cockroach, and I won't pretend to be anything else."

Miss Cockroach learned her lesson, and from that day onwards she always wore black, and learned to work hard and be sensible and live simply, with her father, in the crack in the kitchen wall. And that is why you will never see a cockroach wearing an aubergine cloak with almond slippers, and you'll never find a silly one, either.

The Giant Okab

There was once a young Persian silk spinner called Yusof, whose mind spun dreams while his fingers spun the soft silk threads.

"I'm not going to sit here for ever doing this dull work," he told himself. "One day I'm going to see the world."

Carefully, he saved all the money he earned and put it away in a leather bag. When the bag was heavy with the weight of gold, he said goodbye to his father and mother and off he sailed to Arabia.

As soon as the ship docked, Yusof jumped ashore and began to explore the town, admiring mosques and palaces, peering down interesting alleyways and listening to strange music from behind closed doors. Quickly he found himself a room in a pilgrim's hostel, and was soon sitting in the inner courtyard with a cool drink in his hand and the chatter of other travellers all around him.

But suddenly, just as it was time to look for some dinner, a violent wind sent the dust whirling round in furious eddies, the trees of the courtyard flailed about as if a hurricane had struck, and everything went dark.

The khan's owner dashed out of his kitchen.

"Run, sirs! Run for shelter!" he shouted.

"The Giant Okab is coming!"

Everyone scattered to hide in their rooms, but Yusof had left his bag of money on the far side of the courtyard, so he darted across to fetch it.

Before he knew what was happening, a vast bird swooped down out of the sky. Its beak was made of brass and was as long as five men laid end to end, and its wings were the size of a ship's sails.

Its iron claws were as sharp as spears, while its feathers were made of hard, glittering copper.

One swish of the creature's wings sent Yusof tumbling to the ground, and a second later the Giant Okab had snatched him up in its claws, which cut deep into Yusof's flesh so that he cried out in agony.

"Put me down!" he managed to shout. "Aah! Stop!"

The Giant Okab snapped its brass beak, making a hideous clanging sound.

"You coward," it screeched, in a voice that grated like metal dragged over rocks. "Accept your fate like a man. Tonight is the twelfth full moon of the year, and you are the sacrifice I must take to the Land of the Demons."

"Take someone else. Don't take me!" pleaded Yusof.

"Who? Who shall I take?" thundered the Giant Okab.

Yusof couldn't think of anyone. He didn't know a soul in this strange land.

"Please," was all he could answer. "I'm young, and my whole life is before me. Let me go."

The Giant Okab hovered for a moment with Yusof in its grasp.

"I'll let you go," it said, "if you promise to give me your son on the day of his wedding."

Yusof wasn't married, and he had no children, so this was an easy thing to promise. "My son?" he said, almost laughing with relief. "Oh yes, you can have my son!"

The Giant Okab dropped him as if he had been a sack of corn, and Yusof, bruised and bleeding, thanked God for his lucky escape.

Yusof travelled on for a year and day, seeing enough wonders to satisfy all his dreams. Then, homesick at last, he returned to Persia. He took up his old trade of silk-spinning, did well, and married a beautiful girl. A year later they had a son and called him Mohsen, and the following year a daughter called Zohreh was born.

Mohsen was a happy little boy. Everyone liked him. He played with the merchants' sons in the town and with his friend the shepherd's daughter in the desert, while Zohreh his sister grew up as pretty as a rose. Their father Yusof prospered and the family lived in great comfort.

When Mohsen was twenty, his father and mother arranged a marriage for him with the daughter of a rich merchant.

"When shall we have the wedding?" Yusof's wife asked him.

"Whenever you like," said Yusof.

"The day of the twelfth full moon, I think," said Yusof's wife, happily looking forward to the wonderful dishes she would cook for the wedding feast.

Yusof wasn't listening. He was calculating in his head how much the wedding would cost. He had quite forgotten the Giant Okab and the promise he had made.

Mohsen's wedding day came. The house was filled with laughter and excitement as guests crowded into the garden. The merchant's daughter arrived in her bridal gown and veil, and though she looked proud and spoilt, Mohsen was excited and happy in his silk and velvet wedding suit.

The musicians struck up their songs. The feast began.

Then, all of a sudden, a wild wind sent the dust whirling upwards in huge spirals, the trees in the courtyard tossed violently about, and everything went dark.

As the guests looked up into the sky, a vast bird swooped down. Its huge brass beak snapped with a hideous jangle, and the beat of its gigantic wings was like the clatter of heavy chains. Its copper feathers grated as its claws reached out to strike. Everyone shrieked, but the loudest scream of all came from the bride.

"The Giant Okab! It's the Giant Okab! Whatever did you do to offend it, you fool?" she yelled at Mohsen. "I'll never marry you now!"

And she pushed through the crowd and ran away.

Yusof suddenly remembered the promise he'd made many years before. Frozen with horror, he watched as the Giant Okab seized poor Mohsen in its claws.

The young man's screams of terror brought him back to life and he dashed forwards and threw himself on the ground.

"Take me!" he shouted. "Sacrifice me to the Demons, only let my son go!"

The Giant Okab tossed Mohsen aside, and a second later its fearsome claws were drawing streams of blood from Yusof's chest.

But Yusof's wife could not bear to hear her husband's shout of pain.

"Let him go! Take me!" she called out.

The Giant Okab dropped Yusof and sank its claws into her shoulders, and she gasped and cried out in agony.

Then, before anyone could stop her, Mohsen's sister Zohreh ran forwards and begged to be taken instead of her mother, but when she too screamed with the pain of the great claws ripping through her skin, the Giant Okab let her go.

Mohsen by now had picked himself up and summoned all his courage.

"You came for me, and I'll go with you," he said bravely, but before the Giant Okab could seize him, a ragged young girl threw herself right into the huge bird's claws. Though pale with fear, she never uttered a sound as the Giant Okab's talons gripped her, and a second later the wind whipped through the courtyard again as the bird's great wings beat and it lifted its victim up into the sky.

"Who was that girl?" the wedding guests asked each other, looking up into the sky in pity and admiration as the Giant Okab disappeared with the girl held in his talons.

"Look! It's coming back!" someone shouted, and the guests began to run about, desperately looking for somewhere to hide. Only Mohsen and Zohreh had the courage to watch and wait.

To their amazement, there was no roaring wind this time. The Giant Okab floated slowly down to earth and set the girl down gently. She lay still and pale, but her eyes were open, and though she was bleeding from her many wounds, not one sound came from her, not even the slightest whimper of pain.

Mohsen and Zohreh ran over to her.

"Don't I know you?" Zohreh began. "Aren't you…?"

But Mohsen was staring at the giant bird. He grabbed his sister's arm. "Look!" he cried. An unearthly light was filling the courtyard and the three of them watched in astonishment as the Giant Okab's copper feathers melted into each other, and its wings grew transparent and disappeared.

The brass beak shimmered and shrank until it was no larger than a bowl. The claws fused together and became a shining sword.

A moment later, a handsome young warrior, dressed as a knight in chainmail with a brass helmet on his head, stood before them.

He knelt beside the ragged girl.

"You have saved me from an evil curse," he told her.

She looked up at the knight, and as she smiled, Mohsen saw that in spite of her old, ragged clothes she was the most beautiful girl he had ever seen.

"What curse?" she asked the knight.

"When I was a child, I killed a sparrow," he answered, "and the King of the Birds laid this terrible spell on me. Every year, on the night of the twelfth moon, I have had to take a sacrifice to the Land of the Demons. The only person who could break the spell was a human being who would bear pain and had no fear of death."

"But why did you let yourself be taken?" said Mohsen, lifting the girl to her feet. "Why did you want to save me?"

"Don't you recognise me?" she answered. "I'm your childhood friend, the shepherd girl. I loved you when we were children and we played together in the desert, and I love you still. I didn't mind dying for you."

Mohsen's parents and all the wedding guests had come hurrying out of their hiding places.

"What's happened?" they were asking. "Tell us!"

So Mohsen told them everything. Then he took the shepherd girl's hand and said, "This is my wedding day, but the girl you chose for me has run away. I've found a bride worthier than her, one who truly loves me, and I'll love her for the rest of my life."

So Mohsen married the shepherd girl. They lived happily ever after, and there was always plenty of butter on their bread.

Kayvan the Brave

A long time ago there was a weaver's apprentice called Kayvan. He was a big lad with broad shoulders and long legs, who knew nothing of the great wide world beyond the weaving shop and the little house he shared with his mother. He sat all day and worked at his loom, and in the evening he went home, ate the supper his mother had cooked and went to bed.

One day, as he worked away, throwing his shuttle to and fro, he caught sight of two mice nibbling at the cloth he was making. He was so startled that the shuttle shot out of his hand, flew through the air and hit both the mice at once, killing them on the spot.

The other apprentices, who liked to tease Kayvan, began to stamp and cheer.

"Wa-hey!" they cried. "Did you see that? What a warrior! What a man!"

And they began to chant:

"Kayvan the brave
with his arrow and bow
killed two lions
with only one blow."

Kayvan, who believed everything he was told, blushed with pleasure and pride.

"You're in the wrong job, my son," one of the apprentices said, winking at the others. "An archer, that's what you should be. Out hunting. In the desert. A talent like yours is wasted here."

"Really? Do you really think so?" Kayvan said .

"A hunter! Of course! Yes, yes!" the others chorused, laughing behind their hands.

Their words lit a fire in Kayvan's heart. He stood up and left the weaving shop, not even stopping to lift his jacket from its hook, and ran straight to the bazaar. There he bought himself a bow and a set of arrows.

The bow was a good one, fine and strong, and the arrows were straight and sharp, but Kayvan frowned. Something was missing. At last he realised what it was.

"I want you to write on this," he said, handing the bow back to the shopkeeper.

"Write? What?" said the man, surprised.

Kayvan squared his shoulders and said proudly:

> *"Kayvan the brave*
> *with his arrow and bow*
> *killed two lions*
> *with only one blow."*

The shopkeeper stared at him respectfully.

"Two lions, eh? Yes, sir. At once, sir!"

When the work was done, Kayvan hitched the bow over his shoulder and marched off into the desert to look for game. On and on he went until, tired and thirsty, he saw a stream with a tree bending over it. He stopped and took a long, cool drink.

It was shady and pleasant by the stream.

"Even a great hunter needs to rest now and then," he told himself, and he hung his bow and arrows in the tree, lay down and fell asleep.

A little while later, a captain of the Shah's cavalry came trotting by. He stopped to look at Kayvan, then saw the bow and arrows in the tree.

MORE FAIRYTALE COLLECTIONS FROM AROUND THE WORLD

Stories from the Billabong
James Vance Marshall
Illustrated by Francis Firebrace

Set against the colourful backdrop of Francis Firebrace's
illustrations, James Vance Marshall lovingly retells
ten ancient legends of the Yorta-Yorta people.
Here you can discover why Kangaroo has a pouch
and just what it is that makes Platypus so special.

The Great Snake
Stories from the Amazon
Sean Taylor
Illustrated by Fernando Vilela

From trickster jaguars to spine-tingling giant serpents,
Sean Taylor's retellings provide a sparkling glimpse
into Amazon people's beliefs and way of life.
Dramatic woodcuts by Fernando Vilela help bring to life
the world's most amazing river.

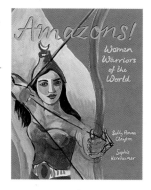

Amazons!
Women Warriors of the World
Sally Pomme Clayton
Illustrated by Sophie Herxheimer

Interspersed with Sophie Herxheimer's vivid paintings,
Sally Pomme Clayton's exciting tales from all over
the world conjure women warriors who kill dragons,
travel to the Northern Lights and learn that warrior skills
are worthless without love.

Frances Lincoln titles are available from all good bookshops.
You can also buy books and find out more about your favourite titles,
authors and illustrators on our website: www.franceslincoln.com